www.mascotbooks.com

A Cavalier Cat: The Story of Pretzel, A Much-Loved Stray from UVA

©2018 Barbara W. Morin. All Rights Reserved. No part of this publication may be reproduced, stored in a retrieval system or transmitted in any form by any means electronic, mechanical, or photocopying, recording or otherwise without the permission of the author.

All University of Virginia indicia are protected trademarks or registered trademarks of University of Virginia and are used under license.

For more information, please contact:
Mascot Books
620 Herndon Parkway #320
Herndon, VA 20170
info@mascotbooks.com

CPSIA Code: PRT0918A
ISBN-13: 978-1-68401-578-8

Printed in the United States

This book is dedicated to my granddaughter, Katie Hammond Young, who graduated from the University of Virginia in 2010 and made this book possible. She has memorialized our family's story about a very special relationship with a cavalier cat.

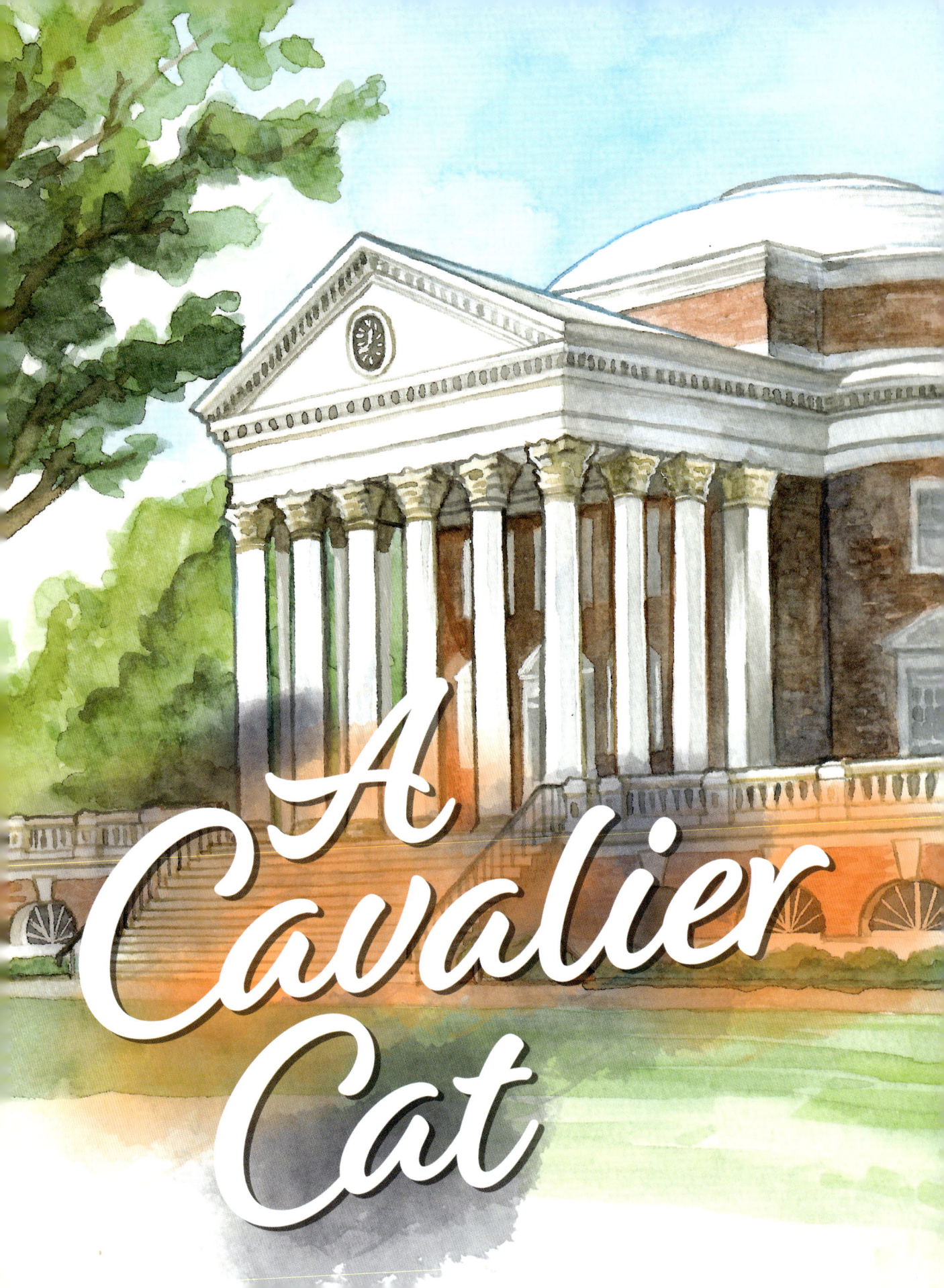

It was a cold December day in Charlottesville, and Professor Morin was surprised to see a hungry-looking cat inspecting the nooks and crannies of his office at the University of Virginia. You see, Professor Morin was busy grading students' papers and really didn't have time for a stray cat. However, this cat liked Professor Morin immediately, so he plopped his tired body on the windowsill behind the desk and napped for the rest of the afternoon.

As Professor Morin assigned the last grade, the cat yawned lazily from its perch. *Maybe it would be nice to have a cat again…for the children,* Professor Morin thought. He was fond of the cat he had when he was a boy. After putting on his jacket, he carefully tucked his new friend in the hood. He trusted that the cat could maintain his balance for the bicycle ride home.

Professor Morin pedaled quicker than usual, excited to introduce his new friend to the family. There was only one thing that might be a problem: Mrs. Morin thought cats were aloof and not to be trusted. A dog, unfortunately, would be a more suitable pet.

Just as Professor Morin walked into the house, the cat poked his orange head out of the hood. Mrs. Morin laughed as the cat curiously looked around.

"I've brought a guest," Professor Morin said.
The children—Jayne, Annette, and Eddie—were thrilled.

"Mommy, can we keep him? He won't be much trouble… he'll wash himself," they begged.

The cat looked up hopefully. And that convinced her. A new family member was added to the household.

After feeding the cat milk and some leftover tuna salad, the next task was to give him a name. Mrs. Morin noticed how he curled his head and tail around his body as he rested after his meal. She decided he resembled a large, yellow pretzel. The family agreed.

The children loved everything about Pretzel: his playfulness, his curiosity, his cleanliness, and especially how he seemed to understand what they said to him. Every night Pretzel had the choice of whose bed he would share.

Jayne wanted him because he made an excellent foot warmer.

Annette liked the way he slept on her pillows.

Eddie loved how loud Pretzel's purr could be.

During his first checkup, the vet determined that Pretzel had been born the previous spring and declared him to be part domestic short-haired and part Siamese. The vet noted his yellow tiger markings, eye color, and his long legs and tail. He was going to be a fine cat!

It was not long before the family, neighbors, and students remarked how handsome Pretzel was becoming, now that he had regular healthy meals and loads of loving attention. They were impressed with how clean he kept himself and how proudly he strutted around Charlottesville.

One Friday evening at the end of winter, Pretzel wasn't at the door when it was time to come in for the night. The children awoke the next morning and searched the entire day. Annette carefully looked for a trail of paw prints on the snow-covered ground. Mrs. Morin made "Lost Cat" signs, and Professor Morin tacked them on the telephone poles on Rugby Road and around the Grounds. The search continued all weekend throughout Charlottesville and UVA®, but Pretzel was nowhere to be found.

On Monday morning, as students were filing into class, Professor Morin spied a yellow shadow weaving between their legs…it was Pretzel!

"That's my cat!" exclaimed Professor Morin. "He's been lost all weekend."

"He's been at our fraternity house and must have followed me to class," said one of his students.

Of course, Pretzel was not really lost. He had found Professor Morin for a second time. He jumped on the professor's desk and quickly fell asleep. The students thought the cat had a lot of nerve, because it was known around the university that no one ever dared to fall asleep in Professor Morin's class!

In the following years, Pretzel became a valuable buddy to the children who were now his family. Annette found him to be a great comfort during thunderstorms. Her grandmother warned her that animal fur might attract lightning, but Annette refused to believe it. When she first heard a thunder clap, she would find Pretzel and hold him close until everything was calm again. Jayne and Eddie loved playing with Pretzel because he never scratched or hissed at them, even if they accidentally pulled his tail. He would simply take refuge under the bed.

When the family moved to another part of Charlottesville, Pretzel never had any difficulty adjusting to his new surroundings. He acquired a favorite activity, accompanying Professor and Mrs. Morin on their evening walks. He always remained at their heels and would sit with them as they chatted with Professor Snavely, a very old neighbor who lived on the next street. Professor Snavely always said, "I've known many cats in my life, but that's the only cat I've seen who thinks he's a dog!"

One spring, Charlottesville sponsored a pet contest at McIntire Park and ribbons were to be awarded for outstanding specimens. Many children came with their pets. There were turtles, hamsters, dogs, puppies, and kittens, but very few adult cats. Annette knew that Pretzel would not be easy to hold in her arms during the judging. He would be curious and eager to size up the other contestants, and besides, he was heavy! But Pretzel understood how important it was to stay calm and allow Annette to properly show him to the judges. He even allowed them to measure him!

What a surprise it was when a judge pinned a blue ribbon on Pretzel and presented Annette with a card that read "The Longest Cat." Their picture was even featured in *The Daily Progress*.

When the Morins drove out of town to visit family, they always took Pretzel along. He became a traveling cat! He liked to sit on the backseat between the children or on top of the suitcase in order to see the road behind him. People in other cars would often wave and say, "Hi Morris!" thinking he was Morris the Cat, a famous feline who advertised tuna.

Visits to Nanny Grace in Durham, North Carolina, were a family favorite. Pretzel even memorized the way! Whenever they approached the Cornwallis Road exit, Pretzel would jump up and meow excitedly. What fun it was to explore Nanny Grace's yard, porch, and large house filled with old things.

Pretzel's long legs and tail provided the strength and speed necessary to make him an excellent hunter. He frequently left a prized catch on the back porch at the door—a chipmunk, bird, or field mouse and sometimes even a pigeon or headless squirrel! Mrs. Morin found these unwanted gifts both amusing and disgusting. As she gingerly disposed of each prize, she reasoned that was what cats do. She considered Pretzel their big game hunter. One time in his pursuit of a blue jay, the family watched him run only on his hind legs while swiping fiercely in the air an inch from his target, which had the benefit of wings. Lucky blue jay... *Pretzel missed!*

Each summer the Morin family spent a few weeks at their beach cottage on Topsail Island, North Carolina. Pretzel liked snoozing on the open windowsill with the ocean breeze ruffling his fur. At night, he loved walking the beach at low tide and chasing sand-fiddlers into their holes.

The children were ready for their walk one evening, but Pretzel did not come when they called him. Surely he would appear at the door in the morning, they thought. When they did not find him in the morning, they began a search of each cottage on the island. Nothing. They combed the inland nearby. Nothing. Professor Morin drove his car slowly up and down the streets of the island. *Still nothing.*

For two days they looked around porches, under house stilts, and under boardwalks. The family realized he might be gone for good this time. Eddie feared Pretzel had been washed away by the high tide. Jayne thought he could have been hurt fighting a wild animal, but Annette said he was a good fighter and worried he had been hit by a car.

Professor Morin reminded the family that they must return to Charlottesville the next day. This made everyone very quiet as they packed their suitcases for the trip home. That night, the children whispered prayers for Pretzel to be safe, wherever he was. "Goodnight, Pretzel. We will dream of you." The tears dried on their cheeks and sleep came.

As hours passed in the black night, a scratching noise broke the stillness. Then more scratching and a loud thud.

Meow...meow...MEOW...MEOW...MEOW!

Pretzel was trying to get in! Everyone dashed to the door and in jumped the most excited cat anyone had ever seen! Constant, breathless meows gradually changed to very loud purrs as the family embraced him in one big hug.

The Morin family had many more wonderful years with Pretzel. He lived to the wise old age of fourteen and spent many days strolling around Charlottesville with the Morin family. Pretzel was a special cat, and he always knew it. He bound their family together. He was happy to receive their love, and he loved them with his whole heart in return.

About the Author

Barbara Wagner Morin and her husband, Dr. Bernard "Bernie" Arthur Morin, moved to Charlottesville, Virginia, in 1965 when Dr. Morin joined the faculty of the McIntire School of Commerce at the University of Virginia. Professor Morin was a McIntire faculty member for his entire academic career and was appointed Assistant Dean in 1971 and Associate Dean in 1974. Bernie also served as Associate Provost for Public Service from 1985 to 1987. He retired in 1998 after 34 years of service.

Barbara W. Morin earned an undergraduate degree from Duke University in Early Childhood Education and a master's in Counselor Education from the University of Virginia. She authored *A Cavalier Cat* to remember her husband, who passed away in 2017, and their special relationship with Pretzel and the University of Virginia.

The Morins have had two children and four grandchildren graduate from the University of Virginia, with hopefully many more to follow.